II0638618

GAME ON!

STRIKE OUT THE SIDE

BY BRANDON TERRELL

www.12StoryLibrary.com

12-Story Library is an imprint of Peterson Publishing Company and Press Room Editions.

Produced for 12-Story Library by Red Line Editorial

Photographs ©: Shutterstock Images, cover

Cover Design: Nikki Farinella

ISBN
978-1-63235-051-0 (hardcover)
978-1-63235-111-1 (paperback)
978-1-62143-092-6 (hosted ebook)

Library of Congress Control Number: 2014946093

Printed in the United States of America
Mankato, MN
October, 2014

TABLE OF CONTENTS

CHAPTER 1

LOCAL BOY HITS IT BIG

Logan Parrish checked his watch for the umpteenth time that afternoon. He could have sworn the minute hand had stopped working.

"I'm so excited I think I'm gonna throw up," his friend Annie Roger said.

She sat beside him and clutched an 8x10 color photo of Jasper Holt against her chest.

Logan placed both hands on her shoulders and gently turned her away from him. "If you're going to hurl, please aim it toward Mason."

"Hey." Ben Mason stepped back, nearly bumping into the boy standing behind them in line.

Logan laughed. Then he checked his watch. *Again.* "When is Jasper Holt going to show up?" he asked.

"Any second now," Annie answered impatiently.

The three friends—along with most of Grover Lake—were standing in the middle of Mega-Sports, an enormous sporting goods store in the east wing of the Grover Lake Mall. The crowd had gathered that day for an autograph signing for Jasper Holt, a baseball player who grew up in town and had recently been drafted by a Major League Baseball team. He was now honing his pitching skills in the minors, playing for a Double A team named the Lawton Catfish.

The crowd in front of them began to murmur and shuffle forward. Logan, who was tall enough to see over most of the crowd, stood on his tiptoes. Sure enough, Jasper Holt had arrived. People clapped. Some cheered. One woman yelled out, "Marry me, Jasper!"

"Hey, we're just in time," Logan heard Carter Cressman say from behind him. He turned to see Carter and Gabe Santiago—the remaining members of their group of close friends—strolling over. They held bottles of water in their hands.

"Refreshments for all," Gabe said, passing out the beverages.

"None for me," Annie said. "I don't want to spill any on my photo of Jasper."

Logan rolled his eyes.

The line slowly began to move forward. Logan was going to have Jasper sign a baseball he brought with him. He reached inside his coat pocket and brought out the scuffed ball. He wrapped his fingers around it, fingering the stitching as if he was getting ready to pitch.

When they reached the front of the line, and Logan was standing before the local celebrity, he was uncharacteristically tongue-tied. Jasper sat at a long table, looking up expectantly.

"Uh . . . hi," Logan said.

"Hey," Jasper replied. "What's your name, pal?"

"I'm, uh, Logan."

"Can I sign that for you, Logan?" Jasper nodded at the baseball in Logan's hand.

"Oh. Yeah. Please." He handed over the baseball. Jasper scribbled his name on it with a Sharpie.

"So . . . what position do you play?" Jasper asked him.

"Pitcher."

"Cool." He handed the ball back to Logan. "Keep those batters guessing."

"Thanks."

Annie shoved past Logan and slapped her photo onto the table. "Hi," she said. "I'm a *huge* fan."

Jasper laughed.

Logan waited while the rest of his friends had their items signed. Then they stood together and snapped a photo with Jasper Holt on one of their phones.

As they walked back through the crowd of people still waiting for an autograph, Logan spied someone they knew. "Hey, there's Sal," he said.

Sal Horton was a large, barrel-chested man with wispy hair, a gray beard, and a wide smile. He owned the kids' favorite shop in town, Sal's Used Sporting Goods. Sal always had a knack for knowing just the thing to help Logan and his friends out when they were struggling at a sport.

Standing next to Sal was his son, Patrick. Patrick looked very much like his father, but his beard was brown and he wore a pair of thick-framed glasses.

"Sal!" Annie waved as their group dashed over to the two Hortons.

"Hello!" Sal's voice was booming, even in the crowded confines of Mega-Sports.

"Isn't Mega-Sports kind of enemy territory, Sal?" Logan said with a smile.

Sal chuckled. "Not at all. I sell mostly used sports equipment," he said. "Besides, I couldn't miss a chance to see Jasper Holt."

"I went to high school with him," Patrick explained. "He was a few years younger than me, but we played ball together. He was good, pitching for the varsity team when he was in ninth grade."

Whoa! Logan thought. He couldn't imagine pitching against high school seniors.

"And I was fortunate enough to be his coach for a time," Sal said. "It's just wonderful to see how well he's doing. Hard work and persistence pay off, kids."

The line began to move again, and Sal and Patrick took a few steps forward. Logan and his friends said goodbye, and then made their way out of Mega-Sports, back into the mall, and off to the food court for a bite to eat.

CHAPTER 2

BRINGING THE HEAT

Logan rolled the baseball around in his fingers. Not the Jasper Holt signed ball. That was in a square plastic case on his shelf at home. This was a brand new, fresh-out-of-the-wrapper game ball, and Logan was staring down the leadoff batter for the Montego Sharks.

It was the first game of the season, and Logan was the starting pitcher for the East Grover Lake Grizzlies. Logan took a deep breath, went into his windup, and fired a rocket down to Gabe, the Grizzlies' catcher.

Thwack! The ball smacked into Gabe's glove.

"Strike!" shouted the ump.

Logan had a wicked fastball. He used all of his might on every pitch, smoking the ball past batters before they ever saw it leave his hand. The batter for the Sharks shook his head, adjusted his blue helmet, and stepped back into the batter's box.

"Come on, Logan," Ben said from his spot at third base. He smacked his fist into his glove. "You got this guy."

Logan sent another rocket toward home. The batter swung, but he was too late—and his bat caught nothing but air.

"Strike two!"

Gabe didn't even bother giving Logan a sign or trying to switch things up. Logan only had one trick in his bag, and it was working.

Thwack!

The bat never left the hitter's shoulder.

"Strike three! You're out!"

The crowd cheered, and Logan heard Annie let out an ear-piercing whistle. She held up a sign with a giant "K" written in black marker on it.

The next two batters were dealt a similar fate as the first. One watched the third strike go past, and the other tried to make contact but failed.

Logan walked back to the dugout with a smile on his face.

The Grizzlies were not a power team.
Instead, they liked to play "small ball," hitting
singles and advancing runners on bunts and
steals. Ben led off, dropping a bunt down the
third base line and legging out the throw.

"Great wheels, Ben!" Coach Santiago
shouted. Logan's dad used to coach the
Grizzlies, but this season he'd passed the
reins over to Gabe's dad, his assistant.

Carter hit next. He sent the ball right
down the line, past the Sharks' diving third
baseman. Ben slid safely into third, and
just like that the Grizzlies had a runner in
scoring position.

Gabe stepped up next, stinky socks
and all. Logan thought his friend's crazy
superstitions were hilarious. Gabe wore

the same "lucky" pair of socks for every game, and he made sure his mother never washed them.

They probably haven't seen the inside of a washing machine in years, Logan thought.

Gabe hit a towering fly ball to right field. He was out, but the ball went deep enough for Ben to tag up from third and score. Next, Tyler Murphy, the team's lanky first baseman, hit a triple, scoring Carter all the way from first.

At the end of the inning, the Grizzlies had notched three runs and led 3-0.

For four innings, Logan mowed down the Sharks. His fastball was on target. The Sharks *did* manage to squeak out a few hits, though, and score a run in the third.

It wasn't until the fifth inning that Logan's stellar game came screeching to a halt.

CHAPTER 3

A TIRED ARM

"How are you feeling, ace?" Coach Santiago walked over to the end of the bench, where Logan was massaging his right arm. The muscles were stiff, and he was losing steam.

"Feeling great, Coach," Logan said. He wasn't entirely telling the truth, but he was stubborn and wanted to get back out on the field, to pitch all seven innings.

Coach Santiago eyed him up and down. "All right."

On the field, the Grizzlies' left fielder, Grayson, hit into an inning-ending double play. Logan stood, slid on his glove, and jogged out onto the field to take the mound.

The leadoff batter jumped on Logan's first pitch, knocking a solid single into center field. The next batter did the same, sending a single into right. The following Shark plated both of them with a massive shot off the wall in right-center. The one after that hit a chopper right over Ben's head at third.

Finally, Gabe jogged out to the mound and peeled off his catcher's mask.

"Everything all right, man?" he asked, wiping the sweat and matted hair from his forehead.

"I'm fine," Logan snapped back. He snatched the ball out of Gabe's catcher's mitt and slammed it into his own.

"Okay," Gabe said. "Shake it off, then. You got these guys, *amigo*."

He jogged back to the plate. Logan looked over at the dugout to gauge Coach Santiago's reaction. Coach was standing with his arms crossed at his chest, staring at Logan.

Logan turned away.

Gabe's right, he thought. *You've got these guys.*

As the next batter stepped into the box, Logan leaned forward. He rolled the ball around behind his back, ready to give the guy another heater across the plate.

Suddenly, Gabe wriggled four fingers.

A changeup? Logan really didn't know how throw a changeup. He shook off the call and prepared to throw another fastball.

He wound up, checked the runners at first and third, turned, and threw.

Crack!

Logan's head dropped. He didn't even watch the ball, but he knew by the crowd's reaction that the home run landed somewhere outside Grover Lake's city limits. The Sharks' players rounded the bases, and their entire team was waiting for the home run hitter as he stepped on the plate.

Logan turned his back on them. Out of the corner of his eye he saw Coach Santiago coming out of the dugout, walking toward the mound. Logan took off his glove and tucked it under one arm.

Stick a fork in me, Logan thought. *I'm done.*

He'd given up 5 runs to the Sharks, who now had a 6-5 lead.

Coach Santiago placed a comforting hand on Logan's shoulder. "They figured you out, kiddo," he said, not angry or upset. Just matter-of-fact. "You'll get 'em next time."

"Yeah," Logan mumbled.

He received a warm round of applause from the crowd as he walked off the mound and back toward the dugout. Coach Santiago called for Max to take his place.

Logan walked into the dugout, which was covered on three sides by wooden walls, out of sight of the bleachers. He chucked his glove to the ground, causing a swirling plume of dirt to rise around it. He kicked it under the bench and sat down heavily.

Max gave up another pair of runs, and Logan could only watch as the Grizzlies dropped their first game of the season by a final score of 8-6.

And it was all my fault.

CHAPTER 4

CAN'T CATCH THE CATFISH

"And now, the starting pitcher for the Lawton Catfish, number 29, *Jasper Holt*!"

The crowd at Lawton Field erupted in a frenzied roar as the announcer called out Jasper's name. Fans clad in Catfish blue and gray rose to their feet. Rock-and-roll music blared from the ballpark's sound system as the starting pitcher walked out to the mound for the first time.

"Go Jasper! Wooooo!" Logan and his friends joined the crowd. They stomped their feet along to the beat of the music.

Logan's dad had scored them a row of seats along the third base line for the first Catfish home game of the season. "There's no way we're missing Holt pitch his first game," his dad, a lifelong baseball fan, had declared.

Now, Logan, Annie, Gabe, and Ben—along with Logan's dad and his older brother, Elliot—were watching the game.

The Catfish were playing a team called the Boulder Valley Outlaws. As Holt threw his warm-up pitches, Logan looked out across the field. Though he was still sore—both mentally and physically—about the game the other night, watching the Catfish was just what he needed to forget about that rough loss.

Maybe Jasper Holt will teach me a thing or two.

And Jasper put on one amazing class in pitching. The Outlaw batters couldn't figure him out. He painted both corners of the plate, throwing accurate fastballs and changeups that twisted up batters and caught them looking instead of swinging. Plus, he had the nastiest curveball Logan had ever seen.

Over the course of the first five innings, Jasper Holt struck out ten batters.

In the middle of the fifth inning, as the Catfish were coming up to bat, Logan said to the others, "I'm gonna go get a hot dog. Anyone wanna join me?"

"Yeah," Annie said, "I'll go."

They shuffled their way out of the row of seats and climbed the steps to the nearest concession stand. As they went to stand in line, a voice behind them said, "Well, fancy seeing you guys here."

Logan spun on his heel to see Sal Horton. Sal was decked out in Catfish apparel and carrying a large bucket of popcorn.

"Hey, Sal!"

"Jasper seems to be pitching one heck of a game today, doesn't he?"

Logan nodded. "He's outstanding. I've never seen a curveball like that. I wish I could pitch that way."

"Someday, perhaps. When you're older. How was your first game of the season?"

Logan's shoulders slumped. "Not good. I was doing fine for a few innings, but they eventually caught up with my fastball and knocked in a few runs."

"Oh," Sal said, "I'm sorry."

"Thanks," Logan said.

"Tell you what. Stop by the store tomorrow, Logan. Any time in the morning, if that's good for you. Patrick and I will be there doing inventory."

"Sure. Do you guys need help?"

"No, but I'm thinking I can help you." Then Sal added, "And bring your glove."

"Sure thing, Sal," Logan said.

After loading up with hot dogs and peanuts and soda, Logan and Annie went back to their seats. Jasper Holt wound up striking out 14 batters and throwing a complete game shutout.

Through it all, the only thing rolling around in Logan's mind was Sal's offer.

He couldn't wait for tomorrow.

CHAPTER 5

THE MAN IN THE PHOTO

Logan leaned forward on his bike, the cool spring breeze blowing in his face, carving his way downhill to the middle of Grover Lake.
He passed the Lake Diner, a barbershop, Fuller Fridges, and a few other local businesses. Ahead of him, he could see the brick building with the orange awning and the plate-glass window sign that read SAL'S USED SPORTING GOODS.

It was midmorning, and the sun was burning the dew off the grass. It was going to be a beautiful, warm day. Perfect for baseball. Logan wondered what Sal wanted to talk with him about.

As they had walked back to their seats at the Catfish game last night, Annie had asked if she could also meet at Sal's, and Logan had said, "Of course." As he cruised along the sidewalk, past the hardware store, he spied her placing her own bike into a rack next to the store.

"Hey, Annie," he said as he screeched to a stop, his back tire sliding off to the side.

"Hi, Logan." She swiped her baseball glove off the front handlebars.

Logan dismounted and lifted his bike into the rack beside hers. Together, they entered the shop. A bell jingled lightly as they pushed the door open. The shop smelled of dust and leather.

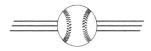

Sal was perched in his usual spot, behind a glass counter filled with signed baseballs and footballs and framed photos of famous athletes. He wore an old Catfish baseball cap. He beamed when he saw them.

"Just who we've been waiting for," he said.

"We?" Annie asked.

Patrick poked his head out into the doorway behind the counter, leading to the stairs and a back hallway. "Mornin'," he said.

"I have something I'd like to show both of you." Sal motioned them to step up to the counter. As they did, the shopkeeper slid an 8x10 photograph toward them. It was in color, but faded. In it, a pitcher stood on the mound, in the middle of his windup. His glove was pulled tight to his chest, and his left leg hung in the air as he pretended to deliver a pitch. He was wearing a Lawton Catfish uniform.

"Do you recognize this player?" Sal asked, amused.

Logan stared hard at the photo. *Come to think of it, the guy does look kind of familiar.* Maybe he was a famous pitcher now, someone who'd gotten his start with the Catfish, like Jasper Holt.

That must be it.

But Logan couldn't place him. He shrugged. "No clue."

Sal's smile reached from ear to ear. He winked and tipped his faded old Catfish hat.

His Catfish hat.

It suddenly clicked in Logan's mind. "No way!" He squinted, looking back down at the photo. "That's *you*, isn't it, Sal?!"

Sal stepped back, and with his mighty frame, he mimicked throwing a pitch. He froze in the same position as Young Sal in the photo. "I started for the Lawton Catfish for a full season before being called up to the majors."

Logan was flabbergasted. He looked at Annie. She wore a similar expression.

"You pitched in the majors?" Logan asked.

Sal sighed. "I started one game. Seven innings of shutout ball. Unfortunately, I tore a muscle in my arm that game. Went on the disabled list, and never quite made it back to the big leagues again."

"That's so sad," Annie said.

"Eh, it's not all that bad," Sal said. "I was able to live my dream. Not many people can say that. Plus, now I get to help kids like you." He rapped his knuckles on the glass. "Which is what I'm going to do today."

"Great!" Logan was excited to be getting pointers from someone who had played in the majors. "Could you teach me how to throw a curveball?"

"Better yet," Sal said, stepping out from behind the counter, "I'm going to teach you how to throw a changeup. It's a perfect pitch to pair with your fastball. Plus, your young arm is not ready to throw a curveball."

As he headed toward the door, he called over his shoulder, "Patrick, let's go!" Patrick appeared again, this time carrying a catcher's mask and mitt. As they filed toward the entrance, Sal plucked a metal bat from a display.

"Where are we going?" Logan asked as they exited the store.

Sal smiled. "Why, we're going to show you how to throw a proper changeup." He flipped the sign on the door to read CLOSED.

Then, the foursome headed off down the sidewalk, toward Grover Park.

CHAPTER 6

A NEW PITCH

The large park in the middle of the city was a decent hike from Sal's shop. Still, despite his size and age, Sal clipped along at a pace that had Logan and Annie struggling to keep up. He hummed as he walked, twice waving at cars that honked as they passed.

Among other things, Grover Park featured two baseball fields, an enormous pond and playground, and a basketball court. Each area was filled with children and parents enjoying the beautiful spring weather. One couple sat in the shade of a towering elm tree, reading together. A cluster of teenagers tossed a Frisbee around. And a group of kids younger than Logan and Annie played a game of pickup basketball.

One of the baseball fields was occupied already. When they reached the pitcher's mound of the empty field, Sal tossed a baseball at Logan. "Let's warm up a bit. Then I want to see your fastball."

When they felt ready, Patrick jogged to the plate. He lowered his mask and squatted down. Then he rapped his fist into his dusty mitt. "Gimme the heater!" he shouted.

Logan took a deep breath. He rolled the ball around, gripped it hard, and unleashed a pitch toward home.

It smacked loudly into Patrick's mitt.

Patrick whistled.

Sal nodded. "Impressive. But I'm guessing that's all you're showing batters."

Logan nodded. "It's my best pitch."

"But I bet your arm gets tired pretty quick. Also correct?"

"Yeah."

Sal nodded, and Patrick tossed the ball to him. Sal plucked it from his glove. "A strong fastball is a good foundation for a changeup. Something I learned in the minors." He held the ball in front of him. "Instead of gripping the ball with the tips of your fingers, like you would for a fastball, you want to hold it in the palm of your hand, which will slow it down."

He showed Logan how he pushed the ball into his palm with his last three fingers.

Then Sal went into his windup. He brought his arm up and his leg into the air. Once again, he looked very much like the young Sal from the photo.

"Aim for the bottom of the zone," Sal explained. "And keep the same arm speed as a fastball. It confuses the batter. Got it?"

Logan nodded. "Got it." *I hope.*

Sal passed the ball off to Logan. Annie took a few practice swings and then stepped into the batter's box, ready for whatever Logan had to offer.

He leaned forward. Saw the mitt. Saw Annie in the box, crouched low. Logan held the ball in the palm of his hand and went into his windup.

The ball seemed like it got stuck in his palm. It came out of his hand late and hit the dirt several feet in front of the plate.

"Yikes," Logan said.

"It takes time," Sal said. "Practice."

He did. Pitch after pitch, Logan followed Sal's directions. Nothing. His pitches were erratic. He threw them into the dirt or offered meatballs that Annie teed off on, sending the ball soaring over his head.

"I can't do it," Logan said in frustration.

"Let's take a moment," Sal said. He clucked his tongue, as if he were considering what to say next. "Logan," he finally began, "Major League Baseball has had its fair share of changeup pitchers. Hall of Famers like Tom Glavine and Greg Maddux, who spent time in the minors perfecting their arsenal of pitches, very much like our dear friend Jasper Holt."

Logan nodded knowingly.

Sal continued. "Because of his changeup, in his prime, Maddux consistently led the league in throwing complete games and wins."

Logan couldn't help but be impressed.

"But none compare to Pedro Martinez." Sal spoke the name with awe and reverence. "He had deadly aim with his fastball," he said, sounding now like an excited child with a secret to share. "Batters were so fearful of it that his changeup would catch them completely off guard. Once, he made 17 Yankees whiff in one game. And that same season, he went on to win the triple crown, leading the league in wins, ERA, and strikeouts."

Logan and Annie were in awe.

Sal tossed the ball back to Logan, who caught it easily. "So let's try that changeup again."

Patrick resumed his spot behind the plate. Annie stepped into the box. Logan's mind raced. He thought of Sal's encouraging words, pictured himself as cunning as Pedro Martinez on the mound. He gripped the ball in his palm and went into his motion. At the plate, Annie gripped the bat and stared back at him.

Logan kept his arm movement tight and let the ball fly.

His pitch looked like a fastball, but just for a moment. The ball seemed to hit the brakes as he released it. Annie flailed with the bat at the ball as it dropped into Patrick's mitt like a dead fish.

"Wow! Nice pitch, Logan," she marveled.

From behind him, Sal said, "I think he's got it." Then, with a smile, the shopkeeper removed his Lawton Catfish hat and crammed it onto Logan's head.

"Now, let me show you how to get a little movement on your fastball."

CHAPTER 7

A SINKING SEASON

Grayson was the starting pitcher for the Grizzlies' next game. They were playing the Matheson Beavers. Logan was cool with playing out in right field. He needed to rest his arm anyway. He and Annie had stayed at Grover Park until well after Sal and Patrick had left to reopen the store. He'd worked hard on his pitching—his changeup especially—and was starting to feel more comfortable with it.

I'll be ready for our next game, he thought, *when we face the Newton Lizards.* They had one of the area's best hitters, Brett Frederick, on their team.

"All right, Grizzlies! Let's go!" Coach Santiago shouted before he rattled off the lineup. The Grizzlies were the away team, so they were up to bat first. Logan was down in the lineup, hitting sixth.

The Beavers were a strong team led by an even stronger pitcher. The first three Grizzlies to face him were called out on strikes. Carter swung so horribly at a pitch that the bat flew from his hands and nearly struck Coach Johnson, who stood by third base.

"That's all right," Coach Santiago told them as they all grabbed their gloves and jogged out onto the field. "Keep your heads up. Play solid defense."

And they did. The first Beavers batter hit a chopper to Ben at third. Ben snagged it and threw a long one-hopper over to Ty, who scooped it out of the dirt a split second before the runner reached first.

"Great play!" Annie shouted from the top of the bleachers.

Grayson got the next batter to pop out to Gabe, and the third to hit a towering fly ball to right-center field. Logan tracked it down, shouting "I got it!" and waving off the center fielder, Seth. He caught it steps in front of the fence.

But the day belonged to the Beavers' pitcher. Logan faced him in the top of the second inning, with two outs. He knocked the dirt from his cleats with his bat and stepped into the box. The first pitch was a fastball that Logan jumped on.

Crack!

The ball sliced down the first base line.

"Foul!" shouted the umpire.

The next pitch was a changeup. Logan was *way* ahead of the pitch, swinging and getting nothing but air.

"Strike two!"

He stepped back, shook his head. *Relax*, he scolded himself. *Keep your eye on the ball.*

It did no good. With an 0-2 count, the Beavers' pitcher threw a changeup in the dirt. It was enough to fool Logan though, who swung helplessly at the errant pitch.

"Strike three! You're out!"

In the fourth inning, Grayson finally tired and the Beavers took full advantage. They batted through their order and plated five runs. Coach Santiago brought in Seth as a reliever, but it made no difference. The Beavers—and their pitcher—had the Grizzlies right where they wanted them.

When Carter flied out to center field to end the game, the final score was 7-1.

It was starting to look as if the Grizzlies' season was a sinking ship. Hopefully, when Logan took the hill against the Newton Lizards, he could get the team back on track.

CHAPTER 8

NERVES

"And that's a team-high *fifteen* strikeouts for Logan Parrish! The crowd goes wild!"

Logan stood in his backyard, pretending that he was pitching the game of his life. About 40-some feet in front of him, attached to the side of the Parrishes' tall wooden fence by a couple of clamps, was one of Logan's mom's old yoga mats. A square of tape noted the strike zone, and a slew of baseballs littered the grass around it.

Logan raised his hand, lifted Sal's Catfish hat from his head, waved it at the imaginary crowd, and then bowed.

"Dude, you're out here *again*?"

Logan jumped at the sound of his brother's voice. Elliot stood on the Parrishes' deck, leaning over the railing and looking down at Logan.

"Practice makes perfect," Logan said, slapping his fist into his open glove.

"Yeah, but save some for the game later tonight," Elliot said.

Logan had indeed been spending most of his spare time practicing his new pitch. He'd passed up numerous opportunities to hang out with his friends—drinking milkshakes at the Lake Diner and playing pickup games of basketball. Instead, he had been online watching videos of Pedro Martinez pitch.

"Mom says you need to eat something before your game," Elliot continued. He checked his watch. "You've got about a half hour before we leave for Newton."

Logan tried to enjoy dinner with his family, but he was too excited and nervous about the Grizzlies' game against the Lizards to eat much. He scarfed down a bit of meatloaf and then hurried off to his room to make sure his equipment bag was packed for the game.

The crowd at Newton's baseball field was quite large. Many fans wanted to watch Brett Frederick play. As Logan walked over to the

Grizzlies' dugout and dropped his equipment bag onto the bench, he glanced over at the Lizards. They were lined up along the base line and listening to their coach. Brett Frederick stood head and shoulders above the rest of the team.

He's like Prince Fielder and Frankenstein's monster combined, Logan thought.

"Dude's a beast, isn't he?" Ben said as he joined Logan, who must have been staring down Brett Frederick.

Logan could only nod.

He changed into his cleats and then jogged out from the dugout to take a few warm-up throws. As he did, he heard Annie call out, "Logan! Logan! Over here!"

He turned to scan the bleachers. Annie was seated near Logan's family and waving her hands over her head. She looked terribly excited. That was because Sal and Patrick sat next to her, along with a very special guest.

"Jasper Holt?" Logan hissed. *What is he doing here?!*

The group smiled and waved, Jasper included.

Sal cupped his hands around his mouth and shouted, "Good luck, Logan!"

"Give 'em everything you've got, kid!" Jasper added.

Every nerve in Logan's body tensed and twitched and tweaked. He could feel his breath catching in his throat. It was bad enough that he had to face off against Brett Frederick with a questionable, untested changeup. But to do it in front of Jasper Holt!

I'm so dead.

Logan stepped onto the practice mound along the first base line, toeing the rectangular rubber and trying to calm himself down. He replayed what Sal had taught him over and over in his head.

Logan warmed up as the hometown Lizards took the field. He mostly stuck to his fastball, though. When he *did* try a changeup, it just hung in the strike zone waiting to be hit out of the park.

His nerves were getting the best of him.

And there was no time to settle down. The umpire raised his hands and shouted, "Batter up! Let's play ball!"

CHAPTER 9

ROUGHED UP

Ben led off for the Grizzlies. He sent a fastball deep toward the fence, but the center fielder tracked it down. Next, Grayson struck out swinging, followed by Ty lining a rocket to the third baseman, who just barely got his glove up in time to catch it.

Logan walked onto the field, taking the mound for the bottom half of the first inning.

The Newton Lizards were a speedy, crafty team. They were also patient at the plate, taking their time and waiting for just the

56

right pitch to hit. And if Logan had control of his fastball, that would have been great for the Grizzlies.

However, he walked the leadoff batter on four straight pitches.

As the runner trotted down to first, Logan slapped the palm on his open mitt and tried to focus. He could hear the Grizzlies' fans acting a bit restless, shuffling in their seats. *It's only been one batter, for crying out loud!*

Angry, Logan sized up the runner, and then fired a fastball to the next batter, right down the middle of the plate.

Thwack!

The ball hit Gabe's mitt hard. "Strike!" bellowed the ump.

There. That's more like it.

Logan did it again for another strike. When Gabe called for a changeup by wriggling four fingers, Logan shook him off.

Index finger, amigo, Logan thought. *Fastball coming right up.*

This time, he threw it high and got the batter to chase it.

"Strike three! You're out!"

Logan's nerves settled a bit, and he was able to get the next batter to pop out to Ty at first base.

Then Brett Frederick, hitting cleanup, stepped into the batter's box.

Logan gave it everything in his tank, throwing a fastball high at the intimidating hitter. It wasn't enough. Frederick turned on it, uncorking a hit that soared high over the fence. It landed with a splash in a pond surrounded by tall reeds.

"Touch 'em all!" the Lizards' bench shouted in unison. From the sound of it, they'd gotten pretty used to saying it. Frederick jogged around the bases, smirking at Logan the whole time.

Despite giving up two more hits in the first, Logan was able to pitch his way out of trouble without surrendering another run.

"Way to get out of a jam, guys," Coach Santiago said as the team walked into the dugout. "Let's get those two runs back."

The Lizards' pitcher was strong, though, and instead of getting the runs back, the Grizzlies went down in order. That gave Logan little time to recuperate.

He continued to shake off Gabe's pitch calls, continued to fire rockets like he always had. And though he was able to strike out a few batters, he became predictable. When Brett Frederick came up to bat again in the bottom of the third inning, there were Lizards on second and third base.

Logan's fastball had lost a little steam. Frederick bounced a bullet off the fence, scoring both runners.

By inning's end, the Grizzlies were down 4-0.

He knew what Coach Santiago was going to say even before he said it. "Seth, start warming up," he said. "Logan, I think we should call it a game."

Logan said nothing. He was too afraid to try anything Sal had taught him and too tired to continue throwing fastballs. He sat down on the bench, near his equipment bag. He kicked the bag out of frustration. The bag toppled onto its side, spilling some of its contents.

The tattered old Catfish hat Sal had given him fell into the dirt.

Logan bent over, picked it up, and dusted it off. He ran his thumb along the brim and spotted the tag inside with the initials "SH" on it.

I can't just roll over and give up.

Logan stood. "Coach," he said, "I wanna go out there next inning."

Coach Santiago shook his head. "Sorry, kiddo, but it isn't—"

"Give me just one more inning," Logan interjected.

The fire must have returned to his eyes. After giving him a long, contemplative look, Coach Santiago nodded. "All right," he said, "one more shot."

Logan's heart raced. "Thanks, Coach."

CHAPTER 10

RALLY TIME

"After three and a half innings, the score is Lizards 4, Grizzlies 0." The umpire slid his mask over his face and added, "Batter up!"

Logan toed the rubber. He spun the ball in his hand and felt the stitching with his fingers. He turned to face the batter.

Gabe wriggled four fingers.

A changeup.

In his head, Logan ran through Sal's instructions on how to throw a changeup.

Hold the ball in the palm of your hand. Keep your arm speed the same. He went into his windup and delivered.

The ball glided toward the plate, dropping to somewhere around the batter's ankles. The Lizard hitter swung, but he was way ahead of the pitch.

"Strike one!" shouted the ump.

"Whoa!" Logan heard Ben say from third.

"Way to fool him, Parrish!" Annie shouted from the bleachers.

The Lizard batter was clearly surprised. He shook his head before stepping back into the box.

Gabe pointed down with one finger. Fastball.

Thwack!

"Strike two!"

He had the batter on the ropes now. His heart raced, and adrenaline coursed through his veins. He felt rejuvenated, as if he was facing the first batter of the game again.

With an 0-2 count, Gabe called for the changeup again.

Logan tucked the ball into his palm. He pretended he was in his backyard again, pitching to a yoga mat covered in tape.

He wound up, reared back, and released.

The ball dipped just enough so that, when the batter swung and made contact, all he could manage was a dribbling grounder back to the mound.

Logan scooped it up and threw to first.

The next Lizard batter popped up to the shortstop. The following batter struck out on a changeup.

Three up, three down.

"Great pitching out there," Coach Santiago said. "Now let's get our offense fired up. Whaddaya say, Grizzlies?!"

Logan's pitching was just the spark the Grizzlies needed. In the top of the fourth, they were able to string together a series of two-out hits to load the bases. Then Carter pulled a scorching triple down the line, all the way to the fence, and the bases cleared.

"Grizzlies! Grizzlies!" the crowd chanted. Logan smiled when he saw Sal and Jasper Holt standing and joining in.

Just like that, they were back in the game. The score was 4-3.

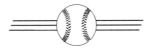

It stayed that way going into the seventh inning. With just one chance left to regain the lead, the Grizzlies came up to bat.

Ty led off. He hit a ground ball to the third baseman, who bobbled the pickup. By the time he threw to first, the long-legged Ty was already there.

The next batter, Seth, walked. The Grizzlies had runners at first and second.

The reliever for the Lizards was having control problems. When the next Grizzly stepped up to bat, he threw a fastball into the dirt. The catcher couldn't handle it, and both runners advanced.

"Second and third with nobody out!" shouted Coach Santiago. "We have the go-ahead run in scoring position."

Unfortunately, the next batter struck out.

Carter was up next. He adjusted his helmet, tapped his cleats with his bat, and stepped into the box.

The first pitch was high. The second inside. Carter was being patient, and now he was ahead in the count. Then the pitcher sent a fastball down the middle of the plate. Carter swung.

Crack!

Logan's breath caught in his throat. The line drive sliced right toward the second baseman. He leapt into the air . . .

. . . and the ball *just* skimmed over the top of his glove.

"Yes!" Logan cheered. "Go! Go!"

Ty scored easily, and Seth hurried to third. The third base coach waved him in.

"It's gonna be close!" Gabe yelled.

The throw came to the plate.

Seth slid headfirst.

"Safe!" shouted the ump.

The Grizzlies went wild. For the first time all game, they were in the lead.

Grayson popped up to end the inning, and the Grizzlies took the field.

"Close it out, boys!" Coach Santiago shouted.

Logan took the hill one last time. Bottom of the seventh. The Lizards' leadoff hitter waited for him. That meant he would be pitching to the top of the order.

And possibly to Brett Frederick.

"Bring it on," he said under his breath.

The first batter chased a couple of changeups and then simply watched as Logan blew a fastball by him.

"Strike three! You're out!" shouted the ump, waggling his thumb in the air. Logan saw Annie hold up her "K" sign. This time, it was turned backward, the sign for a strikeout where the batter doesn't swing.

Two outs away.

The next batter stepped up. He squinted and sneered, and then spit in the dirt. Gabe signaled for a fastball. Logan gave it to him, the ball sizzling right across the sweet part of the plate.

"Strike one!"

The next pitch, a changeup, was fouled off. The next two pitches, Logan tried to get the batter to swing at another off-speed pitch, low and inside, but the kid was patient.

Gabe pointed his index finger down. Fastball.

Thwack!

"Strike three! Two outs!"

The Lizard shook his head in awe. Logan was in the zone.

Until he saw Brett Frederick in the on-deck circle, watching him.

He struck the next batter on the arm with a fastball.

The crowd gasped.

"Take your base," the ump said, pointing to first. The batter shook his arm and trotted down the line.

Then the massive, humongous Brett Frederick stepped up to bat.

Logan got behind in the count quickly. His first pitch was wide. His second low. He wondered if Coach would let him intentionally walk Frederick, so that he could face the next batter. But he looked out at the crowd and saw Jasper leaning forward, watching intently.

I can do this.

Gabe called for a fastball, and Logan zipped one in.

Crack!

The ball shot straight up into the air. Gabe threw off his mask, trying hard to track it down. But it sailed over the backstop, into the bleachers.

"Foul ball!" shouted the ump.

The count was 2-1.

Gabe asked for the fastball. Logan shook it off. Gabe asked for a changeup. Logan nodded.

He caught Frederick by surprise. The big hitter swung for the fence and came up with nothing but air. Logan could have sworn he felt a breeze coming off the bat.

"Strike two!"

2-2. This is it. This is the game.

Logan looked Gabe right in the eyes. Like telepathy, the two knew exactly what to do.

Four fingers.

Changeup.

Perfect.

Logan adjusted his cap, straddled the mound, and eyed up the runner. Then he went into his windup and delivered.

The ball headed for the hitter's sweet spot, waist high in the middle of the plate. Then, suddenly, it broke down, dropping ankle-high toward Gabe's outstretched mitt. Logan saw Frederick's eyes grow wide as saucers. He tried to stop his swing, but it was too late.

Whiff!

"Strike three—*you're out!*"

Frederick peeled off his helmet and threw it to the ground in disgust. "How am

I supposed to hit that?!" He grumbled and cursed all the way back to the dugout.

The Grizzlies rushed the mound. They slapped Logan on the back, congratulating him on a spectacular comeback victory.

"What a changeup," Coach Santiago marveled. "Where did you learn that?"

Logan shrugged. "An old friend." He searched out Sal in the crowd and found him standing and applauding.

The Grizzlies had won their first game of the season. Now, with Sal's help and Logan's newfound skills, the rest of the season was going to be downright amazing.

THE END

ABOUT THE AUTHOR

Brandon Terrell is a Saint Paul-based writer. He is the author of numerous children's books, including picture books, chapter books, and graphic novels. When not hunched over his laptop, Brandon enjoys watching movies and television, reading, baseball, and spending every spare moment with his wife and their two children.

ABOUT THE BASEBALL STARS

Pedro Martinez was a dominant pitcher throughout most of his career, leading his league in ERA for five years and strikeouts for three years.

Years in the Majors: 18 (1992–2009)

Teams: Dodgers, Expos (Montreal), Red Sox, Mets, Phillies

Win-Loss Record: 219-100

Cy Young Awards: 3

Tom Glavine was not a strikeout pitcher, yet he won more than 300 games in his career. He was inducted into the Baseball Hall of Fame in 2014.

Years in the Majors: 22 (1987–2008)

Teams: Braves, Mets

Win-Loss Record: 305-203

Cy Young Awards: 2

Greg Maddux is considered one of the best pitchers of all time, having logged more than 5,000 innings and won 355 games. He was inducted into the Baseball Hall of Fame in 2014.

Years in the Majors: 23 (1986–2008)

Teams: Cubs, Braves, Dodgers, Padres

Win-Loss Record: 355-227

Cy Young Awards: 4

THINK ABOUT IT

1. When Logan was struggling, Sal mentored him by teaching Logan how to throw a new pitch: a changeup. Have you ever had a mentor help you? What were you struggling with? How did the mentor help you, and were you successful afterward? Would you ever consider being a mentor?

2. Imagine you are Gabe, crouched down behind the plate and calling the pitches. What would you do when Logan shakes off your signal to throw a changeup and throws a fastball instead? How would your actions affect the team? How did Logan's?

3. Read another Game On! story. In *Strike Out the Side*, Sal helps Logan with his pitching. Who does Sal help out in the other story, and how does he help? How are Sal's actions similar in each story? How are they different? Use examples from both stories to explain your answer.

WRITE ABOUT IT

1. Do you have any local heroes like Jasper Holt? It might be someone who plays sports or someone who simply has a positive influence on your town or city. Pick your favorite. Describe what that person does and why you consider him or her a hero. Do you hope to follow in your hero's footsteps?

2. Early on in the story, Logan struggles with his pitching. Write about a time when you struggled to do something. What were you having trouble with? How did you overcome your struggles? Did you seek help or find another way to succeed?

3. Pretend you are the sports announcer during one of the baseball games in this story. Write down what you would say during the game. Remember, announcers get quite excited during intense moments.

GET YOUR GAME ON!

Read more about Logan and his friends as they get their game on.

Eyes on the Puck
Goalie Annie Roger learns she needs prescription glasses, and her confidence is shattered. Will a visit to Sal's Used Sporting Goods be enough to help Annie see things differently?

Pass for the Basket
When a new transfer student takes away the spotlight, Ben Mason is frustrated with his role on the basketball team. Will Ben be able to learn the true meaning of leadership?

Race Down the Slopes
Blinded by a crush, Gabe Santiago accepts an invitation to join the ski team even though he has never skied slalom before. Will a pair of goggles from Sal's Used Sporting Goods prove to be Gabe's lucky charm?

READ MORE FROM 12-STORY LIBRARY

Every 12-Story Library book is available in many formats, including Amazon Kindle and Apple iBooks. For more information, visit your device's store or 12StoryLibrary.com.